DUE DATE

MAY 1 3 1993		
JUN 2 4 1993	NOV 1 5 1994	
	APR 0 2 1995	
JUN 0 7 1994		
	AUG 0 2 1995	
JUL 2 7 1994		
FEB 0 7 1995	MAR 0 8 1996	
FEB 0 5 1996	MAR 0 1 1997	
MAY 2 2 1997	JUL 0 7 1997	
JUN 0 6 1997		
		Printed in USA

Dealing with Feelings:

I'm Frustrated

Written by Elizabeth Crary
Illustrated by Jean Whitney

Book Design by John Fosberg

ISBN 0-943990-64-5 Paper
ISBN 0-943990-65-3 Library binding
LC 90-63870

Parenting Press, Inc.
P.O. Box 75267
Seattle, WA 98125

Dealing with

Why a book on frustration?

Parents often ask me for help dealing with their children's feelings. Two factors may contribute to this: (1) Many people were taught to ignore their feelings as children. Now they want to raise their own children differently, but have no idea how. (2) Everyone feels frustrated occasionally—both children and adults. We all need skills to handle our feelings.

How can this book help?

I'm Frustrated can help children accept their feelings and decide how to respond.

The book models a constructive process for dealing with frustration. It shows a parent and child discussing feelings openly. The story also offers specific options for children. There are verbal, physical, and creative ways described to express feelings. In addition, *I'm Frustrated* serves as a role model for parents who wish to change the way they respond to their children's feelings.

How to use *I'm Frustrated*

I'm Frustrated becomes more useful with time and repetition. A couple of readings probably won't make a dramatic change. But you can start to help your child transfer the information to real life.

Distinguish between feelings and actions. Read the book letting the child choose the options. Ask, "How does Alex *feel* now? What will he *do* next?" at the end of each page. More about understanding feelings is below.

Introduce different options. Children need several ways to cope with frustrated feelings that work for them. This story offers ten ideas. When you are done reading, ask your child, "What else could Alex have done?" Record your child's responses on the "Idea Page" at the end of this book.

Use as a springboard for discussing other situations. Begin by discussing something that happened to someone else. Ask your child to identify the feeling and the alternatives the child tried. Talk with your child from the perspective of collecting information, rather than what is right or wrong.

For example, assume a friend, Jenny, was trying to build a tower but the blocks kept falling down. Ask, "How did Jenny *feel* when the blocks fell down again?" "What did she do first when she felt upset?" "What else did she do?" Possible answers: she quit, took a break, cried, or asked for help.

When your child can distinguish between feelings and behavior for other people, you can review something she did in the same non-judgmental way.

Elizabeth Crary, Seattle, WA

Feelings and the Parent's Role

One of your jobs is to help children understand and deal with their feelings. Children need basic information about feelings, they need to have their feelings validated and they need to have tools to deal with those feelings.

Develop a vocabulary. Children may feel overwhelmed or scared by feelings. One simple way to begin understanding feelings is to label them.
- Share your feelings: "I feel frustrated when I can't find my car keys."
- Read books that discuss feelings—for example, the *Let's Talk About Feelings* series.
- Observe another's feelings: "I'll bet he's proud of that A+ grade."

In addition, introduce your child to different words for related feelings—for example, mad, furious, angry, upset, etc.

Distinguish between feelings and actions. Understand that feelings are neither good nor bad. Feeling mad is neither good nor bad. However, hitting is a behavior. Hitting is not acceptable. You can say, "It's okay to be mad, but I cannot let you hit your sister."

Validate the child's feelings. Many people have been trained to ignore or suppress their feelings. Girls are often taught that being mad is unfeminine or not nice. Boys are taught not to cry. You can validate children's feelings by listening to them and reflecting the feeling. Listen without judging. Remain separate. Remember, your child's feelings belong to her/him.

When you reflect the feeling ("You are frustrated that Stephanie has to go home now"), you are not attempting to solve the problem. Reflecting, or acknowledging the feeling helps the child deal with it.

Offer children several ways to cope with their feelings. If telling children to "use your words" worked for most kids, grownups would have little trouble with children's feelings. Children need a variety of ways to respond——auditory, physical, visual, creative, and self-nurturing. Once a child has experienced a variety of responses, you can ask her what she would like to try.

For example: "Do you want to feel frustrated right now or do you want change your feeling?" If your child wants to change you could say, "What could you do? Let's see, you could run around the block, make a card to send to Stephanie, talk about the feeling, or read your favorite book." After you've generated ideas, let your child choose what works for her. Often all children need is to have their feelings acknowledged.

Be gentle with yourself. Remember, some situations are resolved quickly and others take time and repetition. Hold a vision of what you would like for your child and yourself and acknowledge the progress you have made.

Alex sat on the steps, watching his brother and sister. They were practicing for a roller skating race that weekend. He smiled as he watched them zoom back and forth. It looked so easy. He wanted to skate too.

Alex decided to try. He got his sister Vanessa's old skates and put them on. He laced them tight, and then stood up. The skates slid out from under him. He landed smack on his bottom.

Alex carefully tucked both feet under himself and tried to stand. The skates slipped again. "How am I ever going to learn to skate if I can't stand up?" he wondered.

He crawled over to the fire hydrant and slowly pulled himself up. He stood for a moment and then fell again. He started to cry, "I can't do it. I can't do it. I can't do it."

Mom came out and asked, "What can't you do, Alex?"

"Roller skate. These skates don't like me. Every time I try to skate, I fall down," he complained.

"You want to skate, and you're frustrated you can't stand up. Is that right?" Mom asked. Alex nodded yes. "Can I help?" she offered.

"I don't know," Alex answered. He felt tight inside — like he might cry. "I want to smash the skates to pieces and throw them away."

"It's okay to feel frustrated, Alex, and I can't let you hurt the skates. What else could you do?" Mom asked.

What do you think Alex can do?

Listen to your child's ideas. If no idea is suggested, continue.

"I don't know," Alex replied.

"Well, I can think of eight ideas," said Mom. "You could—

That's a lot of ideas. What will you try first?"

What do you think Alex will try first?

Turn to the page your child chooses. If no idea is suggested, continue the story.

Ask Someone for Help

"I want some help," Alex decided.

"What kind of help do you want?" Mom asked.

"Someone to help me up and hold my hand so I don't fall," Alex replied.

"Sounds like you know what you want. Who do you think can help you?" Mom asked.

"Vanessa or Charlie," Alex replied. He wanted his sister or brother.

"Here they come. You can ask them," Mom replied.

"Charlie," Alex called out, "help me skate!"

"Okay, I'll help you skate down to Johnson's and back," he answered. Alex hung onto Charlie as they skated. Each time Alex fell, Charlie helped him up. Charlie explained how to bend his knees to keep balanced. By the time they got back, Alex could stand up by himself, but he was still very frustrated.

What do you think Alex will do next?

Sit and cry . . . . page 12
Talk about his feelings . . . . page 16

Sit and Cry

Alex fell down a couple more times and then gave up. "It's not fair," he sobbed. "The skates hate me. Everybody can skate but me."

He cried and cried.

After a bit Mr. Wilson, a neighbor, noticed Alex crying and came over. "Are you okay?" he asked.

"Yes. No. I don't know," Alex sniffed. "I want to skate but I keep falling down."

"Sounds like you feel so frustrated you decided to cry," Mr. Wilson replied. "Sometimes crying helps and sometimes it doesn't. If it doesn't help, you might take a break or talk to someone about your feelings."

What do you think Alex will do?

Take a break . . . . page 14
Talk to someone about his feelings . . . . . page 16

Take a Break

"I've had enough," Alex said to himself. "The more frustrated I get, the more I fall. I had better find something fun to do before I explode or turn black and blue from bumps."

"Now what would feel nice?" he asked himself. "Playing with my kitten would be nice. So would reading a book. I don't know which to do."

"I know," he said, as he pulled a penny from his pocket. "I'll toss a coin. Heads, I'll read. Tails, I'll play with my kitten." He tossed the coin. "Heads!" he said. He picked up the penny and went inside.

He got his favorite book. Then he sat down in the big chair and curled up with a blanket. "Now this is nice," he said, as he opened his book. "I feel warm and cozy now."

When he was done reading, Alex decided he was ready to practice again. He put on the skates and tried to skate to the tree.

Each time he tried, he fell. "This isn't fair," he cried. "I am so mad I could scream."

Turn to page 16.

Talk about Your Feelings

Alex took off the skates and went to find his mom again. "Mom, every time I try to skate, I fall down," he complained. "Even when someone helps me, I fall down. I want to practice, but my frustrated feelings get so big I feel like I'll blow up. What can I do?" Alex asked.

"That's a good question," Mom answered. "Everyone needs to find ways to calm themselves, whether they are mad, frustrated or scared. I can think of two ideas.

"You could blow out the frustrated feelings. "Or you can do something physical, like running around the block. Lots of times when feelings get too big, you can make them smaller by doing something very active.

"Those are two ideas. If you need more, let me know."

"Thanks, Mom. I know what I'll do," Alex answered.

What do you think Alex will do next?

Do something physical . . . . page 18
Blow out the frustrated feelings . . . . page 20

Do Something Physical

"I am going to run," Alex decided. "It won't help me skate, but it will help me feel better," he thought. "How far do I have to run?" he asked his mom as he sat down to take off the skates.

"I don't know," she answered. "With each person it's different. I suggest you run until you feel tired — and then run a little bit more."

"Here I go," he said, as he charged off. He ran around the block, and then stopped to see how he felt. "Hey, Mom," he called. "It worked. I don't feel frustrated now."

He sat down to put on the skates and try again.

If Alex gets frustrated and wants to try something different, what do you think he will try?

Blow out the frustrated feelings . . . . page 20
Reward yourself for trying . . . . page 28

Blow Out Frustrated Feelings

Alex decided to do something different. He asked his mom, "How does blowing out the feelings work?"

"You breathe in deeply, and then let your breath out slowly. As you breathe out, imagine the frustrated feelings going out with the air. Many people find it easier to imagine if they close their eyes and relax their bodies."

"Can I do it with the skates on?" he asked.

"Yes," Mom replied, "but I suggest you sit down. Otherwise you might slip while you concentrate on your breathing."

Alex took a deep breath, thinking, "In comes the clean air." Then he closed his eyes and let it out slowly, thinking, "Out goes the bad air."

He repeated the chant to himself as he breathed, "In comes the clean air, out goes the bad air. In comes the clean air, out goes the bad air." After a little bit, he stopped to check how he felt. "Hmmm, I feel quiet inside," he said to himself. "The frustrated feelings are almost gone."

Turn to page 22.

Find Out How Other People Calm Themselves

Alex saw Mr. Wilson planting bulbs in his flower garden. He took off the skates and went over. He watched him pull weeds for a couple of minutes, then asked, "Mr. Wilson, do you ever get frustrated?"

"Sure, son. Everyone does."

"But you never look mad or upset," Alex protested.

"True. When I was a boy, I was frustrated a lot, until I learned to calm myself down."

"How do you do that?" Alex asked.

"Well, if it's something that is going to take a long time, I imagine how good I will feel when I am done, and then chart my progress as I go."

"But Mr. Wilson, what do you do if you get frustrated anyway?"

"I paint. I pretend the feelings slide from my body onto the paper. Later when I am not so frustrated, I think about how I can do it better."

What do you think Alex will do?

Ask what 'chart progress' means . . . . . . page 24
Paint a picture . . . . page 26

Chart Your Progress

"What does 'charting your progress' mean?" Alex asked his neighbor.

"It means recording your improvement. First, you make a goal. Your goal is what you want to do. What *do* you want to do?" Mr. Wilson asked.

"I want to skate up and down the block like the big kids," Alex replied promptly.

"That's a good goal, but kind of big for a starting goal," Mr. Wilson said. "Can you think of a smaller goal?"

Alex thought a moment and then pointed, "Skate from the steps to that tree. What's after making the goal?"

"Then you count the number of falls it takes you to skate to the tree. Write the number down. After a couple of trips, the number will get smaller and you can see you are making progress," he explained.

"Come on," Mr. Wilson said. "I'll help you get started." Mr. Wilson counted the falls—1, 2, 3, 4, 5, 6. "Six falls on that trip. Now skate back."

Alex skated back and forth while Mr. Wilson counted. Finally Mr. Wilson said, "Alex, look at your progress. You made ten trips. Now you can skate to the tree and only fall once or twice."

Turn to page 28.

Paint a Picture

Alex decided to draw his feelings. He took off his skates and ran in the house. "Mom," he called, "can I use the paints? Mr. Wilson says painting sometimes helps him get unfrustrated."

"Sure," Mom replied. "They're in the cupboard over the washing machine. Remember to put down newspaper to protect the table and floor."

At first Alex smeared black and red paint all over the paper. Next he took another piece of paper and splattered lots of colors. Finally he took a new sheet of paper and painted a picture of three kids skating together.

"Look, Mom," he said. "This is Vanessa, Charlie, and me skating together. And you know what? Painting works for me too. I feel happier now. I'm going to go out and try to skate some more."

Turn to page 30.

Reward Yourself for Trying

After Alex had practiced a couple more times, he was ready to quit. He watched as Vanessa skated over to him. "Stopping so soon?" she asked.

"It's not fun to fall down all the time," he answered sadly.

"I know. And it is part of beginning to skate. Everyone falls when they learn," Vanessa explained. "You have to keep practicing or you'll never learn."

"How do you keep from quitting?" Alex asked.

"I make goals and reward myself," Vanessa answered.

"You mean a goal like skating to the tree and back five times?"

"Yes. Then reward yourself. Mom said we can have an ice cream cone, or read a book, or something."

Alex thought a moment and decided, "I will skate to the tree five times and then get an ice cream cone."

He continued to skate and fall, skate and fall. Finally he made his last trip. "Yippee!" he cried. "I did it. Now for an ice cream cone."

Turn to page 30.

For the rest of the day, Alex worked very hard at letting go of the frustrated feelings and learning how to skate. By supper time he could skate two or three houses away without falling. "Look at me, Mom. I can skate," he called.

"That's wonderful," his mother said.

"I feel great," Alex declared smiling. "I can skate now. *And*, I know what I can do if I get frustrated again."

The End

Idea Page

Alex's ideas:

- Ask for help
- Sit and cry
- Take a break
- Talk about your feelings
- Do something physical
- Blow out your frustration
- Ask others how they calm themselves
- Chart progress
- Paint a picture
- Reward yourself

Your ideas:

- Take a deep breath
- Walk away
- Count to ten or higher
- go to the spot
- be grateful
- ask others how they calm down

Teach Children Social Skills!

The Children's Problem Solving books by Elizabeth Crary help children learn social skills by letting them make decisions for the characters and then see the consequences.

These books are different! They are fun, game-like books, rather than traditional "sit- quiet" books. As one young child remarked to a friend, "You get to pick what happens. If you don't like what happened, you can go back and try again."

This series helps children **learn about feelings and behavior** in an easy, non-threatening way. The series *(32 pages, illus., 10×8, $4.95 each)* includes:

I Want It: What can Amy do when Megan has the truck she wants?

I Can't Wait: How can Luke get a turn on the trampoline?

I Want To Play: How can Danny find someone to play with?

My Name Is Not Dummy: How can Jenny get Eduardo to stop calling her a dummy?

I'm Lost: What can Amy do to find her dad at the zoo?

Mommy, Don't Go: What can Matt do when he doesn't want his mother to leave?

FREE BOOK OFFER! Buy five problem solving books and get one free! A $29.70 value for only $24.75—order today!

Lets Talk About Feelings:
Nathan's Day at Preschool
By Susan Conlin & Susan Levine Friedman

Follow four-year-old Nathan throughout a day full of feelings. Children share with Nathan mixed feelings as he says goodbye to his mom, pride in the picture he's making, anger when his friend crashes into him on the swing set, and feeling loved when he thinks about his parents.

Grownups accept Nathan's feelings and guide his behavior when needed.
32 pages, 7×8 ½, $4.95 paperback, illus.
